HANUMAN

ramah sastra-bhrtam aham

"Of wielders of weapons I am Rama."

—BHAGAVAD-GITA, 10.31

HANUMAN

based on Valmiki's RAMAYANA

Paintings by Li Ming

Retold by Erik Jendresen and
Joshua M. Greene

TRICYCLE PRESS
Berkeley, California

Listen now while I tell you a tale of a time long past when the world was menaced by a ten-headed beast whom the gods could not control. He was called Ravana: *He who makes the universe scream.*

ONCE, when he was young, Ravana sat on a mountaintop and became so still that he stopped the winds that move the planets and keep the universe alive. The gods begged him to rise from his place, but Ravana would not move until he was promised protection from gods and demons, the mightiest forces of creation. In his pride, he did not ask for protection from men or monkeys. So the gods granted his wish, and Ravana rose up from his place, and the planets moved and the universe breathed.

But Ravana was now all-powerful, and soon he trained his army of warriors—the savage Rakshasas—to take what they wanted and to destroy anything in their path.

The gods prayed to Vishnu, the Lord of all Creation—but now only a man or a monkey could stop Ravana from crushing the universe.

My name is Hanuman. I am a monkey and, like all children, I was born with great powers.

When I was little I wanted to be a hero, but it was very hard to stay out of trouble. I was curious, and forever hungry, so I was always finding the hidden vats of honey and eating the great piles of fruit that the elders saved for feast days.

Then one day I looked up and saw the Sun and thought that it was the biggest, brightest, ripest, most beautiful fruit I had ever seen.

So I jumped to snatch it.

Up I went, higher and higher, for three full days—that is how wonderful my powers were then! And just when I was about to reach out my hand to pick the Sun from the sky, Indra, god of the Heavens and the Rains, flew by on the back of his great elephant.

Remember that I was very young, and the elephant looked to me like a big fruit with a long nose! So I chased Indra and his flying fruit, but this made the god angry and he struck me with a thunderbolt.

And back to earth I fell.

I broke my chin when I landed, and that is when I was given my name, Hanuman, broken chin. But that is not all. As I lay in my mother's arms and my chin began to heal, the adults of my village prayed for me to forget the wonderful powers of my childhood.

And so it was that I forgot the magic with which I was born. I grew up to become Commander of the Monkey Army, but I had no memory of the things that I could do.

Then something happened that changed all history.

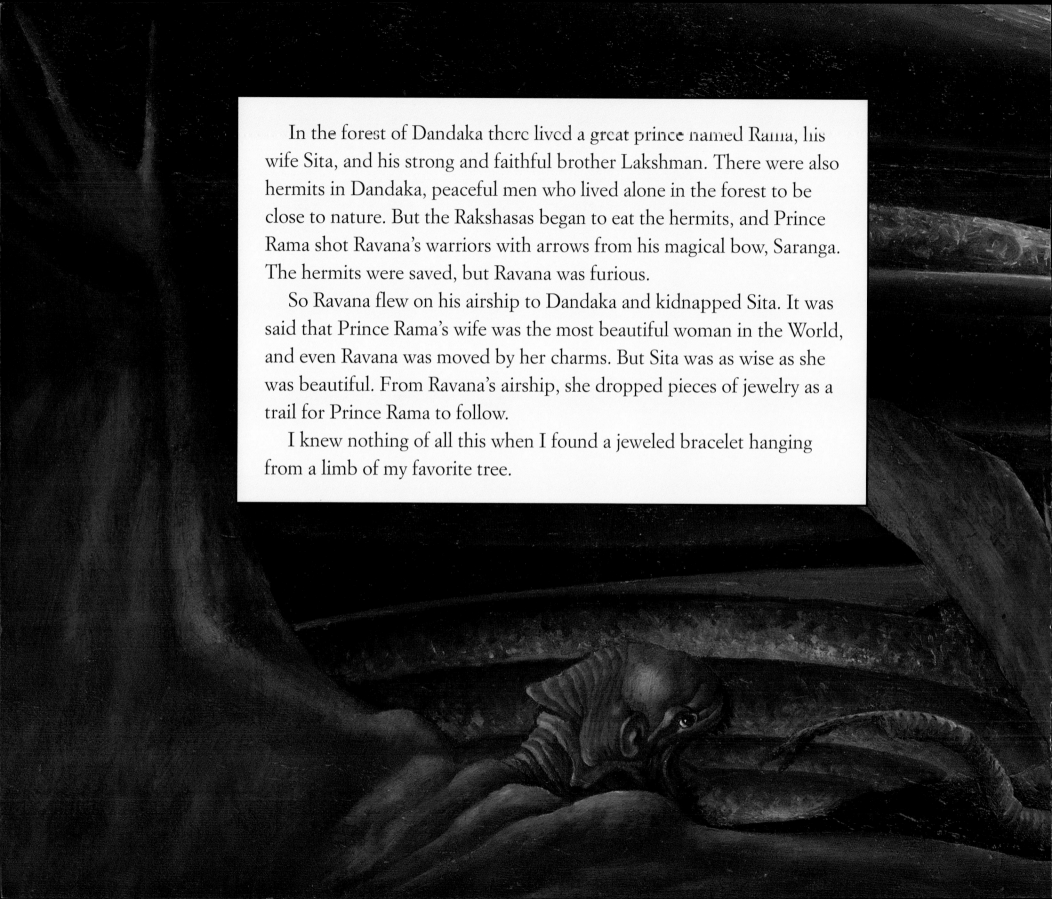

In the forest of Dandaka there lived a great prince named Rama, his wife Sita, and his strong and faithful brother Lakshman. There were also hermits in Dandaka, peaceful men who lived alone in the forest to be close to nature. But the Rakshasas began to eat the hermits, and Prince Rama shot Ravana's warriors with arrows from his magical bow, Saranga. The hermits were saved, but Ravana was furious.

So Ravana flew on his airship to Dandaka and kidnapped Sita. It was said that Prince Rama's wife was the most beautiful woman in the World, and even Ravana was moved by her charms. But Sita was as wise as she was beautiful. From Ravana's airship, she dropped pieces of jewelry as a trail for Prince Rama to follow.

I knew nothing of all this when I found a jeweled bracelet hanging from a limb of my favorite tree.

The name Rama means *He who gives great happiness,* but when he walked into our village looking for his lost wife, he was the saddest creature I had ever seen. Prince Rama's love for Sita was like the love of the Sun for the Earth, but there was no light in his eyes now and his face was twisted with grief.

He spoke to Sugriva, King of the Monkeys, and I listened as he described Sita and the jewels that she wore. When I stepped forward with the bracelet in my paw, Prince Rama fell to his knees.

"Who are you, my friend?" he asked.

"This is Hanuman," said King Sugriva. "He is the Commander of my forces."

Prince Rama looked deep into my eyes and placed his hands on my shoulders.

"Will you help me?" he asked.

I nodded, watching the tears that fell down his cheeks.

Monkey search parties would travel north, east, south and west to look for any sign of the kidnapped princess. The south was unexplored, so I would lead that party through wild jungle and treacherous mountains to the edge of the ocean. My friend Jambavan, the human King of the Bears, would join me.

Before we left, Prince Rama held my paw in his hands.

"You can do more than you know," he said. And he gave me his ring. If I found Sita, the ring would prove that I was his messenger.

Adventure? Yes! But it was more than that. I knew how it felt to break my chin, but I could only imagine the pain of a broken heart. Finding Sita would heal Prince Rama's heart, and that was why we set out to find the lost princess.

The search parties to the north, east and west returned empty-handed to the forest. By the time my party reached the ocean, we were tired, bruised and beaten by our adventures to the south. Jambavan and I stood on the ocean's shore and peered out across the water to a city like a golden mountain rising through the mist to touch the clouds.

This was Lanka, Ravana's island fortress many miles from shore. It was where he stored the treasures he took from the worlds he conquered, and it was our last hope.

But how to get there? Monkeys can jump, to be sure, but...

It was Jambavan who reminded me of Prince Rama's last words: "You can do more than you know, Hanuman," he said. He pointed to my crooked chin. "When you were a child you jumped to the Sun itself."

And I remembered.

I remembered why I had come this far. I remembered the sorrow of Prince Rama's face and the hope that glistened in his eyes.

And I jumped.

And I remembered the powers that were within me, all the magical powers of my childhood. Hideous sea creatures snapped at my feet, and the waters rose up to drown me, but I jumped above them all.

I was older when my feet touched the ground of Lanka—maybe because I remembered all that I had known when I was young.

The city of Lanka was unlike anything in this world. There were golden towers, jeweled terraces, garden mazes, bottomless lakes filled with lotus flowers, markets piled high with goods from every corner of the universe, and the air was thick with the scent of spices. Slaves and Rakshasas were everywhere, and I knew that Ravana would live somewhere above them all.

So I climbed the highest tower on the island, and there in a garden, standing with her back to a tree, was a woman so beautiful that only a god....

"You!" A voice exploded in the stillness of the tower-top garden and stopped my mind from thinking. I watched as He who makes the universe scream lurched toward Sita as she pressed herself against the tree. "Be my wife or be cut to pieces and eaten for a morning meal!"

Sita looked away, and nine more heads grew suddenly from Ravana's neck, for that is how he showed his anger.

"You have two months in which to decide," he screamed. "Then, one way or another, you will be mine!"

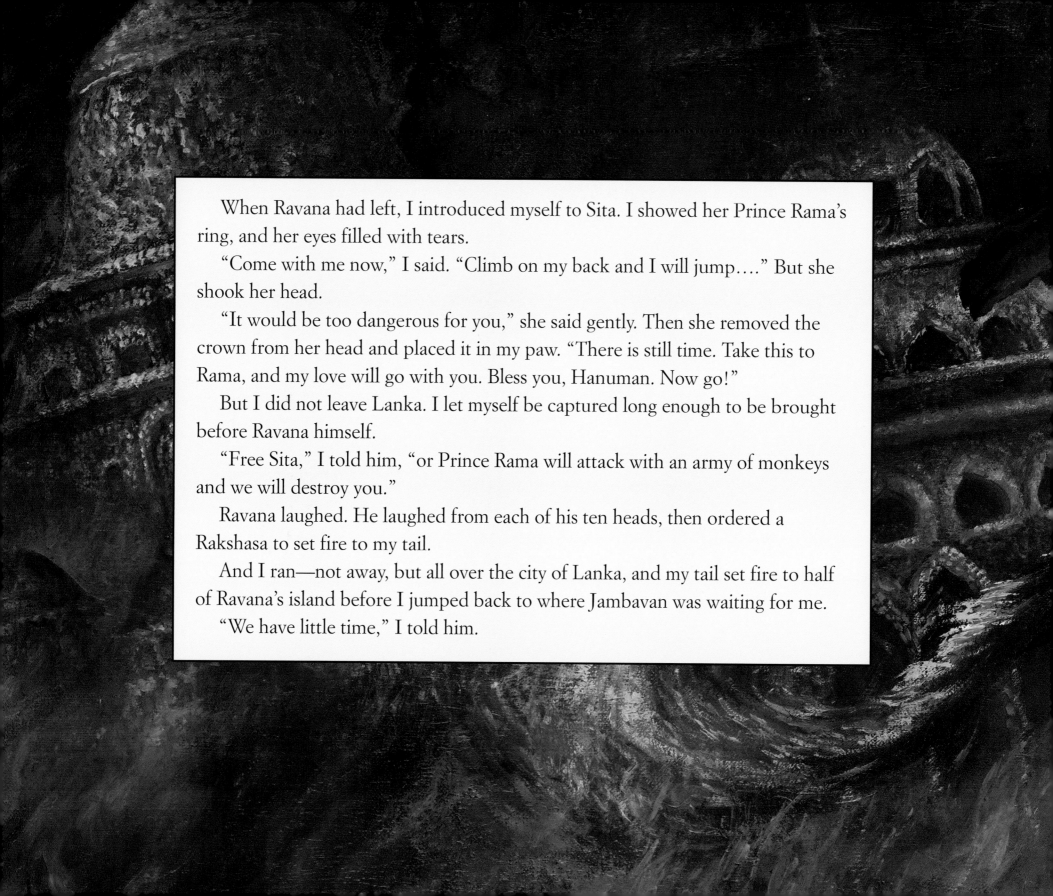

When Ravana had left, I introduced myself to Sita. I showed her Prince Rama's ring, and her eyes filled with tears.

"Come with me now," I said. "Climb on my back and I will jump…." But she shook her head.

"It would be too dangerous for you," she said gently. Then she removed the crown from her head and placed it in my paw. "There is still time. Take this to Rama, and my love will go with you. Bless you, Hanuman. Now go!"

But I did not leave Lanka. I let myself be captured long enough to be brought before Ravana himself.

"Free Sita," I told him, "or Prince Rama will attack with an army of monkeys and we will destroy you."

Ravana laughed. He laughed from each of his ten heads, then ordered a Rakshasa to set fire to my tail.

And I ran—not away, but all over the city of Lanka, and my tail set fire to half of Ravana's island before I jumped back to where Jambavan was waiting for me.

"We have little time," I told him.

Back in the forest, I told Prince Rama the news. When I gave him Sita's crown, he threw his arms around me.

And so it was that Prince Rama, Lakshman, Jambavan and I led an army of men and monkeys back to the shore and stared across the waves to the island of Lanka.

But how to move an army across miles of ocean?

"We will build a bridge of stone," said Rama.

A tiny spider kicked a grain of sand into the water at Prince Rama's feet. I laughed at this puny effort, but Rama scolded me.

"There is no such thing as large or small when it comes to acts of love," he said.

And so it was that man and monkey and spider built a bridge of stone in five days, and our army crossed the sea to Ravana's island fortress.

How to describe the battle of Lanka? In all of history there has never been, nor will there ever be, an army as fierce as Ravana's. His Rakshasa warriors were shape-changing creatures with magical powers. They flew over our heads and hurled weapons that darkened the sky and burned the earth.

Rama and Lakshman split the darkness with great bolts of light and put out the fires with arrows of rain. *What sort of magic did this prince and his brother possess?*

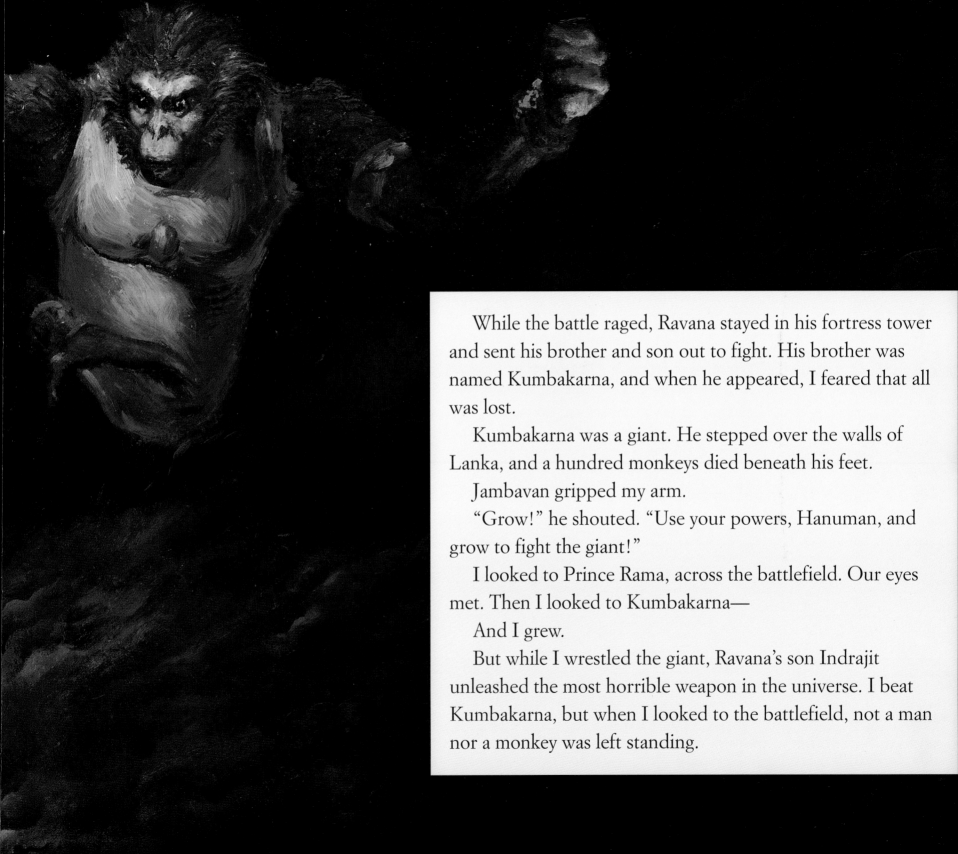

While the battle raged, Ravana stayed in his fortress tower and sent his brother and son out to fight. His brother was named Kumbakarna, and when he appeared, I feared that all was lost.

Kumbakarna was a giant. He stepped over the walls of Lanka, and a hundred monkeys died beneath his feet.

Jambavan gripped my arm.

"Grow!" he shouted. "Use your powers, Hanuman, and grow to fight the giant!"

I looked to Prince Rama, across the battlefield. Our eyes met. Then I looked to Kumbakarna—

And I grew.

But while I wrestled the giant, Ravana's son Indrajit unleashed the most horrible weapon in the universe. I beat Kumbakarna, but when I looked to the battlefield, not a man nor a monkey was left standing.

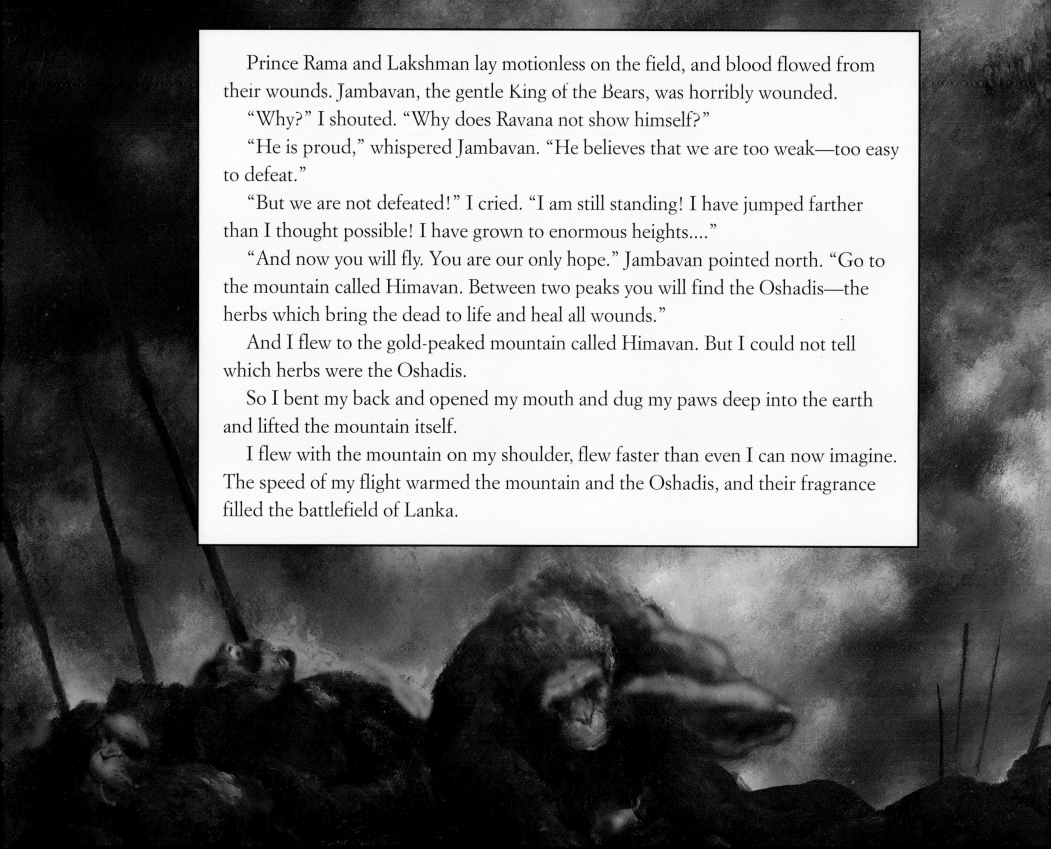

Prince Rama and Lakshman lay motionless on the field, and blood flowed from their wounds. Jambavan, the gentle King of the Bears, was horribly wounded.

"Why?" I shouted. "Why does Ravana not show himself?"

"He is proud," whispered Jambavan. "He believes that we are too weak—too easy to defeat."

"But we are not defeated!" I cried. "I am still standing! I have jumped farther than I thought possible! I have grown to enormous heights...."

"And now you will fly. You are our only hope." Jambavan pointed north. "Go to the mountain called Himavan. Between two peaks you will find the Oshadis—the herbs which bring the dead to life and heal all wounds."

And I flew to the gold-peaked mountain called Himavan. But I could not tell which herbs were the Oshadis.

So I bent my back and opened my mouth and dug my paws deep into the earth and lifted the mountain itself.

I flew with the mountain on my shoulder, flew faster than even I can now imagine. The speed of my flight warmed the mountain and the Oshadis, and their fragrance filled the battlefield of Lanka.

Prince Rama opened his eyes and saw all about him the thousands of monkeys who had died, watched as they rose to their feet and lifted their weapons for battle.

Lakshman rose up and drew his bow and sent an arrow through Indrajit's heart.

Jambavan ran to the head of our army, raised his fist, and the monkeys cheered.

And Ravana looked down from his fortress tower. His brother and son were dead. So Ravana dressed himself in golden armor, and when he stepped onto the field of battle he was the fiercest and most magnificent warrior that man or monkey had ever seen.

Prince Rama chose a single arrow. He chanted a prayer to the Sun, fitted the arrow to the bowstring of Saranga, and let the arrow fly.

Ravana looked into Prince Rama's eyes, and something happened.

I think that Ravana saw that the power of goodness was greater than the power of evil. And at that very moment, Prince Rama's arrow pierced his heart.

And he who made the universe scream fell before a man and a monkey.

Then the gates of Lanka opened. Sita emerged, and with her came the thousands of people whom Ravana had turned into slaves.

And when Sita and Rama touched, peace returned to the universe.

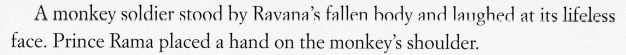

A monkey soldier stood by Ravana's fallen body and laughed at its lifeless face. Prince Rama placed a hand on the monkey's shoulder.

"Do not mock him," he said. "If it were not for his pride, he could have been a god. Give him a hero's funeral."

A wind stirred through the gardens of Lanka, and flower petals fell on Ravana's body. I bowed to Prince Rama.

"Hanuman," he said, "you have shown me more love and friendship than I can ever repay."

I shook my head. "Thanks to you, I have jumped farther than is possible. I have grown to fight a giant. I have flown great distances and carried a mountain on my back."

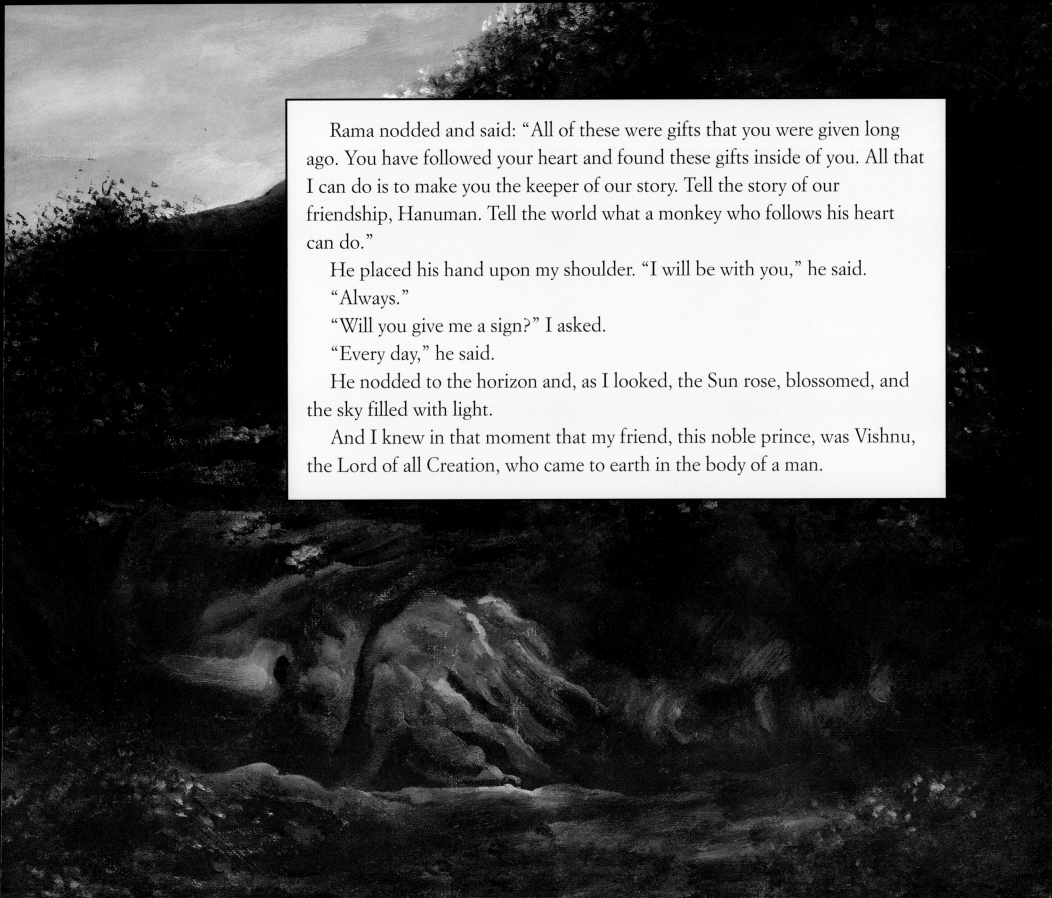

Rama nodded and said: "All of these were gifts that you were given long ago. You have followed your heart and found these gifts inside of you. All that I can do is to make you the keeper of our story. Tell the story of our friendship, Hanuman. Tell the world what a monkey who follows his heart can do."

He placed his hand upon my shoulder. "I will be with you," he said. "Always."

"Will you give me a sign?" I asked.

"Every day," he said.

He nodded to the horizon and, as I looked, the Sun rose, blossomed, and the sky filled with light.

And I knew in that moment that my friend, this noble prince, was Vishnu, the Lord of all Creation, who came to earth in the body of a man.

Rama, Sita and Lakshman left the island of Lanka in Ravana's magical airship.

And I returned to the forest of Dandaka. I was greeted as a hero. All the little monkeys crowded around me. They jumped onto my shoulders and hung from my arms.

"Did you really fight monsters?"

"How many were there?"

"Were you hurt?"

"Tell us, please! Oh, tell us the story!"

And I have been telling it ever since.

AUTHOR'S NOTE

HANUMAN is the monkey-hero of an ancient text called *Ramayana* (The Path of Rama), a scripture held sacred by millions and one of the most translated works of all time. The original was written thousands of years ago by the poet Valmiki in the land we now call India. Valmiki's text contains 24,000 Sanskrit couplets and hundreds of stories. The main text tells of Prince Rama's childhood, his marriage to Princess Sita, their exile to an enchanted forest, Sita's abduction by the demon king Ravana, and Rama's victory in a cosmic battle between his brave monkey soldiers and Ravana's cruel demon warriors. This book is a concise retelling of this great adventure, seen through the eyes of Hanuman as he grows from mischievous young monkey to wise guardian of Rama's story.

To His Divine Grace A.C. Bhaktivedanta Swami Prabhupada —J.M.G.

To Her Divine Grace Savannah Aslee —Bhakta Santa

CONCEPT DESIGN BY IAIN MCCAIG

ADDITIONAL CHARACTER DESIGN BY DHRITI AND RAMDAS

Stories To Remember, P.O. Box 311, Old Westbury, New York 11568

Book design by Mina Greenstein
Additional production by Chloe Nelson

Typeset in Simoncini Garamond

Published by Tricycle Press
a little division of Ten Speed Press
P. O. Box 7123, Berkeley, California 94707
www.tenspeed.com

Library of Congress Cataloging-in-Publication Data
Jendresen, Erik.
Hanuman: based on Valmiki's Ramayana; paintings by Li Ming;
retold by Erik Jendresen and Joshua M. Greene.
p. cm.
ISBN 1-883672-78-3 hc / ISBN 1-58246-125-2 pbk
1. Hanuman (Hindu deity)—Juvenile literature. 2. Valmiki—Adaptations.
I. Li, Ming, 1958– . II. Valmiki. Ramayana. III. Title.
BL1139.5.H36J46 1998
398.2'0954'01—dc21   98–4319 CIP AC

First printing, 1998
First paperback printing, 2004
Manufactured in China
1 2 3 4 5 6 — 08 07 06 05 04